# Gold in the Hills
## A Tale of the Klondike Gold Rush

**By Candice Ransom**

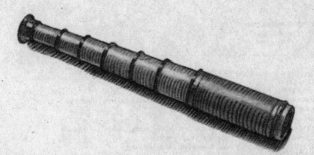

**Illustrated by Greg Call**

MIRRORSTONE

# GOLD IN THE HILLS

Published by Wizards of the Coast, Inc. Time Spies, Wizards of the Coast, Mirrorstone and their respective logos are trademarks of Wizards of the Coast, Inc., in the U.S.A. and other countries.

Cover and Interior art by Greg Call
First Printing: March 2008

9 8 7 6 5 4 3 2 1

ISBN: 978-0-7869-4776-8
620-21554740-001-EN

Library of Congress Cataloging-in-Publication Data

Ransom, Candice F., 1952-
  Gold in the hills : a tale of the Klondike Gold Rush / Candice Ransom ; illustrated by Greg Call.
     p. cm. -- (Time spies ; 8)
  "Mirrorstone."
  Summary: When the magic spyglass transports Mattie, Alex, and Sophie Chapman
to the Yukon Territory during the gold rush, they enlist the
help of author Jack London to track down a boy's stolen sled dog.
  ISBN 978-0-7869-4776-8
  [1. Time travel--Fiction. 2. Gold mines and mining--Fiction. 3. Sled dogs--Fiction.
4. London, Jack, 1876-1916--Fiction. 5. Magic--Fiction.
6. Brothers and sisters--Fiction. 7. Yukon Territory--History--19th century--Fiction.]
  I. Call, Greg, ill. II. Title.
  PZ7.R176Gol 2008
  [Fic]--dc22

                                                                    2007037174

J TM

U.S., CANADA,
ASIA, PACIFIC, & LATIN AMERICA
Wizards of the Coast, Inc.
P.O. Box 707Newport,
Renton, WA 98057-0707

EUROPEAN HEADQUARTERS
Hasbro UK Ltd
Caswell Way
Gwent NP9 0YH
GREAT BRITAIN
+1-800-324-6496Please keep this address for your records

Visit our Web site at www.mirrorstonebooks.com

For Sioux

# Contents

# The New Innkeepers

"We're in charge," Mattie Chapman said to her brother. She took her mother's apron off its hook on the kitchen door. "Dad's too sick to get out of bed. He didn't tell Mom, or she wouldn't have gone to Richmond."

"So we're the innkeepers for the weekend?" Alex asked. "Sounds like a lot of work."

"It won't be so bad." Mattie tied the apron around her waist.

"Are you kidding? You hate to do chores!"

"This is different. We're the bosses." She picked up The Gray Horse Inn appointment book and flipped to the page with the day's date. Then she let out a long breath.

"Don't tell me," said Alex. "We have a full house."

"No. Only one guest tonight." She tried to sound businesslike but she was too excited. "Somebody named Charles Cutright has booked the Jefferson Suite!"

Alex snatched an apple from the fruit bowl and tossed it high in the air. "Yippee! We'll have the new Travel Guide all to ourselves!"

"We have lots to do before he gets here." Mattie handed her brother a dust cloth. "Dust the Jefferson Suite. And make the bed. I put clean sheets on the dresser."

"I thought you said we were the bosses?

How come you're bossing me?"

"Because I'm the oldest."

"By one puny year," he said. "I can't wait till I'm nine and then I can boss you—" He stopped, realizing what he had said.

"You'll always be a year younger than me," Mattie said. "Now go clean the Jefferson Suite." As Alex headed up the stairs, she called out, "And stay out of the tower room!"

Mattie gathered the ingredients for the cookies her mother made every afternoon. She thought about the time they had discovered the secret of the tower room. Earlier that summer, they had moved into this old house in Virginia that their parents had turned into a bed-and-breakfast. The tower room on the third floor hid a secret—a magic spyglass that took the kids on fantastic missions back in time.

Now a new Travel Guide was on his way to stay at The Gray Horse Inn. Travel Guides always started the kids' adventures. Tomorrow morning, she and Alex and their little sister Sophie would be off on an exciting trip. She wondered where they would go this time.

When the shortbread was in the oven, Mattie squeezed lemons for fresh lemonade. Her mother's recipe said to stir in one cup of sugar.

*That can't be right*, Mattie thought, and dumped in three cups.

With the lemonade chilling in the refrigerator, she dashed up to the second floor to check on her father.

Mr. Chapman was lying in bed, the quilt drawn up to his chin. Winchester, their big black cat, was curled up asleep beside him.

"How are you feeling, Dad?" Mattie asked.

"Rotten." His voice was scratchy. "Who

gets the flu in the middle of summer?"

"You do. But you'll feel better soon." Mattie fluffed her father's pillows so he'd be more comfortable. She liked being in charge.

"Maybe you should call your mother and ask her to come home," Mr. Chapman said.

"Mom's been planning to see Aunt Sherri for ages," said Mattie. "We only have one guest tonight. We'll be fine, Dad. Don't worry."

"I don't like relying on you kids, but I couldn't get up if the Queen of England were coming." Mr. Chapman's sneeze shook the bed. Winchester woke up, annoyed.

"Do you need anything?"

"Can you get me a book?" He pointed to the small bookcase by the window. "It's on the end. *Call of the Wild.*"

Mattie found the book. The cover showed

a dog running in the snow. The author's name, Jack London, was printed in letters shaped like icicles. She brought the book over to her father. "What's it about?"

"Oh, it's a great story. It's about a kidnapped dog that is taken into the frozen North." He put on his reading glasses and settled back.

"Call me if you need anything else," Mattie said. "I'd better get back downstairs."

Before she reached the kitchen, she smelled something burning.

The shortbread!

She burst through the swinging door, snatched the oven mitt off the counter and yanked the oven door open. Smoke billowed out. She set the pan of scorched shortbread on top of the stove and fanned the smoke with the mitt.

"Is the house on fire?" Alex skidded into

the kitchen. "Whew! Boy, did you burn the shortbread!"

"It isn't burned," Mattie insisted. "It's just . . . very dark brown."

"You can't serve that stuff to the new Travel Guide. He'll break a tooth!"

"There isn't anything else," she said, beginning to feel panicky. Running an inn wasn't as easy as she'd thought.

The doorbell rang. Mattie rushed down the hall, but Sophie was ahead of her.

"I'll get it!" Sophie cried. "I'm the greeter." She flung open the front door and blurted, "Welcome to The Gray Horse Inn Bread and Breakfast!"

Mattie groaned. Bread and breakfast! What would the guest think?

An elderly man stood on the porch, smiling at her. He had a little white mustache and wore a red bow tie with his crisp blue shirt.

"Hello. I guess I'm at the right place. I'm Charles Cutright."

"Come in," Mattie said in her best inn-keeper voice. "Sign the register, please. Sophie, will you take Mr. Cutright to the Keeping Room?"

Clasping Mr. Cutright's hand, Sophie skipped down the hall to the Keeping Room, where guests relaxed.

Alex came out of the kitchen, carrying the serving tray with a platter of shortbread and the pitcher of lemonade.

"I scraped off most of the burned stuff," he whispered. "Maybe we can get him to talk about our next trip."

"Don't be too obvious," Mattie said. "Travel Guides don't want us to know their real identities, for some reason."

In the Keeping Room, Mattie poured Mr. Cutright a glass of lemonade.

"Are you kids all alone?" he asked.

"Our mother is in Richmond this weekend," Mattie explained. "And our father is—" She paused, not wanting the guest to think the house was full of germs.

"He's sick!" Sophie exclaimed. "Sick as a dog! That's what he said."

"Don't pay any attention to Sophie," Mattie said hastily. "She's only five."

"So, how come you're here?" Alex asked Mr. Cutright. "I mean, what kind of a job do you have?"

Mr. Cutright took a sip of lemonade, then quickly set his glass on the coffee table.

Mattie wondered why he didn't drink more. She tasted the lemonade. It was so sweet, her teeth ached. Maybe she'd added a little too much sugar.

"I'm a historian," Mr. Cutright replied. "I'm writing a book about Thomas Jefferson and the Ordinance of 1784."

"The what of 1784?" asked Mattie.

"It's sort of like a law," he replied. "Jefferson was concerned about the future of the western territories—"

"Thomas Jefferson lived at Monticello," Alex interrupted. "That's only a few miles from here."

"I know." Mr. Cutright picked up a piece of shortbread, looked at it, then put it back on the plate. "That's why I chose your charming bread and breakfast." He winked at Sophie.

"Do you travel a lot?" Alex asked. "And guide people? You know, like on trips?"

Mattie rolled her eyes. Could Alex be any more obvious?

"Not really," said Mr. Cutright. "I've spent the last five years researching this book at my university. It's quite a fascinating time in Jefferson's life. People think of him as the third president and the creator of the Declaration of Independence. But he did so much more."

"He grew fifteen kinds of peas," Sophie put in.

Mr. Cutright looked at her with surprise. "How did you know that?"

"We know a lot about Jefferson," Mattie said. "It's sort of a hobby of ours."

"I bet you don't know about the Ordinance of 1784," Mr. Cutright said. "You see, Jefferson was a member of the Confederation Congress. That was the congress that came into being after the end of the Revolutionary War and after the Articles of Confederation were ratified by all thirteen states."

Mattie glanced at Alex, who pretended to yawn. She was thinking the same thing. The new Travel Guide was a bore.

"You see, the United States was a

brand-new country," Mr. Cutright droned on. "A lot of policies had to be decided on. Like money. What kind of money system would we have? Jefferson wrote a report that we should use dollars instead of British pounds. Thanks to Jefferson, we have dimes instead of shillings!" He chuckled.

Mattie rubbed her eyes. She was tired. It had been a long day of baking and doing laundry and taking care of her father. And she still had work to do that evening.

Mr. Cutright returned to his favorite subject. "Jefferson also—"

Mattie stood up. "I'm sorry, Mr. Cutright, but I have to fix the casserole for tomorrow morning."

"You don't have to go to any trouble for me," he said. "A bowl of cereal will be fine."

"No, we really have to," said Mattie. "Sophie can take you up to your room."

# 2

# Off to Metropotamia?

"Where is the muffin basket?" Mattie grumbled to herself the next morning. She and Alex had stayed up late last night making the egg-and-cheese casserole for this morning. Then she had gotten up at six thirty to bake it and make orange juice. Now she needed the bread basket to heat the muffins in.

Alex pushed through the swinging door. "You haven't set the table yet. It's almost eight o'clock."

She glared at him. "Why don't you set the table?"

"I have to fix the coffee." He filled the coffeemaker with water, then opened the can of coffee. "How much do I put in?"

"Ask Dad." Mattie checked the top of the refrigerator for the muffin basket.

When Alex came back a few minutes later, he rooted around in the utensil drawer for the coffee scoop. Then he turned to Mattie and said, "I don't know if Dad said six scoops or sixteen. He still talks funny."

"Put the most in to be on the safe side," she said. "People hate weak coffee. Where is that dumb muffin basket?"

"Right there." Alex pointed to the rack of copper pans hanging over the stove.

Mattie looked up. The cloth-lined basket was perched on top of a saucepan. Nestled inside the basket was a yellow stuffed rabbit.

"Sophie!" Mattie reached up for the basket, knocking the rabbit onto the counter. She dumped the frozen muffins in the basket, popped it into the microwave, and punched the timer buttons.

"Jingle bells, jingle bells . . ." Sophie's high-pitched voice floated down the hall. "Jin-gle all the way!"

The door opened on the final note as Sophie entered the kitchen. Mr. Cutright walked in behind her. Today he wore a bright blue bow tie with a green shirt.

"Good morning!" he said cheerfully. "Do I smell coffee?"

"Mr. Cutright!" Mattie said. "Um . . . guests don't usually come into the kitchen."

Alex switched off the coffeemaker. "Coffee's ready."

"Good. Can I take some up to your father?" Mr. Cutright poured coffee into a

15

mug. He stared at it the inky liquid.

"I made it nice and dark," Alex said.

"Maybe it's a little strong for a sick man." Mr. Cutright filled the teakettle and plunked it on the stove. "I'll fix him a cup of tea instead."

"Jin-gle bells, jin-gle bells," Sophie sang.

"Sophie, it's summer," Mattie told her. "You don't sing winter songs in the summer. And thanks for hiding the muffin basket."

"You're welcome." Sophie danced her stuffed elephant Ellsworth and the yellow bunny along the counter.

Mattie wondered how her mother cooked a big breakfast every morning. Her father helped, but it was still a lot of work. She felt a twinge of guilt. Setting the table was her job, but she usually forgot and her mother had to do it.

She had just grabbed a handful of knives

and forks when the oven bell dinged. The casserole! She didn't want to burn the main course. She pulled the dish out and slid it onto the hot pad.

Alex wrinkled his nose. "Yuck. Mom's casserole isn't runny. And hers doesn't have eggshells in it."

The microwave buzzer went off. Mattie jerked open the door and pulled out the muffin basket. "Oh no!"

The muffins were hot, but hard as rocks. She must have set the timer too long.

"These would make great ammo!" Alex pretended to hurl a muffin through the window.

Mattie felt like crying. Their one chance to be innkeepers to the Travel Guide and everything had gone wrong!

Mr. Cutright took one look at the lumpy casserole and said, "Too many eggs are bad for the heart anyway. Do you have cereal?"

"Yes." Mattie showed him the cupboard where they kept the cereal and bowls.

"Great." Mr. Cutright shook cornflakes into a red bowl, then sat down at the table where the Chapmans ate when they didn't have guests.

"Wait! I have to set the dining-room table." Mattie snatched up the knives and forks so fast she dropped them with a loud clatter.

"Don't go to any trouble for me," Mr. Cutright said, helping her pick up the silverware. "I'd rather eat in the kitchen. Makes me feel right at home."

Mattie fixed a tray with hot tea and dry toast and carried it upstairs to her father.

"How are things going?" Mr. Chapman rasped.

"Uh . . . Mr. Cutright says he feels right at

home." She decided not to tell him about the messed-up meal.

On her way back down the stairs, she had a sudden thought. Travel Guides ate breakfast in the dining room with the other guests. They also talked to the kids and wrote postcards that they left on the sideboard.

The front of the postcards always changed from a photograph of The Gray Horse Inn to a picture of where they would go on their adventure. The messages would be a hint too.

How could Mr. Cutright write a postcard if he wasn't eating breakfast in the dining room? How would they start their mission?

In the kitchen, Alex was launching orange seeds with his spoon, Sophie was feeding Ellsworth dry cereal, and Mr. Cutright was talking about the Ordinance of 1784—again!

"—Jefferson proposed the ordinance

because he believed the western territories should govern themselves like the thirteen states," Mr. Cutright said. "After the territories had enough settlers, Jefferson felt they should be admitted to the United States as states."

"Really?" said Mattie. "Mr. Cutright, don't you want to finish your tea in the dining room?"

The Travel Guide rattled on. "Jefferson even thought up ten names for these new states. Assenisippia, Cherronesus, Illinoia, Metropotamia, Michigania, Pelisipia, Polypotamia, Saratoga, Sylvania, and Washington."

Alex hooted. "Sylvania! Metropotamia! What a bunch of goofy names! I'm glad they didn't become real states."

"Ah, but three of them did become states," said Mr. Cutright.

Mattie was still worried about how to

get Mr. Cutright to write a postcard. "Are you going to Monticello today?" she asked. When Mr. Cutright nodded, she said, "Be sure to buy a postcard while you're there."

"I will. Jefferson was very interested in exploration of the western territories, but he never traveled farther west than these Blue Ridge Mountains." Mr. Cutright drank the last of his tea. "Well, I'd better be going. I'll leave my check on the hall table."

Mr. Cutright left the kitchen. As the door swung back, Mattie saw him go into the dining room.

"Hey," she whispered to Alex and Sophie. "I think he's going to write a postcard!"

"About time," said Alex. "If I had to hear one more word about the Ordinance of 1784, I was going to scream."

Mattie waited until Mr. Cutright was gone, then sprinted into the dining room.

She grabbed the postcard from the tray.

Dear Herb, Pa and me made it over the Pass. One man carried five crates of cats! We'll come home when we're rich. Mike.

"Crates of cats? That's weird," Alex said. "What's the picture?"

Mattie flipped the postcard over.

"Oh boy!" Alex exclaimed. "We're going sledding!"

"Maybe," Mattie said. "But where?"

"The territory," Sophie said.

Mattie looked at her little sister. "What territory? How do you know?"

"I just do. Last one to the tower room is a rotten egg!" Sophie took off.

Mattie and Alex raced up behind her to the third floor.

Alex swiveled the bookcase-panel that led into the secret tower room.

"Wait!" Mattie said. "Our last Travel Guide gave us a hint about this trip. Remember?"

She ran downstairs to the coat closet and grabbed parkas, boots, hats, and mittens, then hurried back up to the tower room.

"Put this stuff on," she told Alex and Sophie.

Summer sun streamed through the long windows and the room was stuffy. Mattie was sweating by the time she'd tugged her boots on.

Alex took the brass spyglass from the desk, the only piece of furniture in the room. He held it by one end.

Sophie tucked Ellsworth in her parka pocket and grasped the middle of the spyglass.

Mattie clasped the other end. The spyglass tingled and grew warm beneath her fingers.

Strange symbols appeared, and white and gold sparks flickered behind her eyelids.

She couldn't stop thinking about what Sophie had said. Suppose they went to one of Thomas Jefferson's territories the Travel Guide had talked about?

As the floor felt as though it were dropping away, Mattie's last thought was, *What if we go to Metropotamia?*

# 3

# Presenting . . . The Chapman Children!

Mattie felt something cold and crunchy beneath her boots. Chilly air blew against her cheeks. She opened her eyes, then blinked.

Snowy mountains rose in the distance. They were thick with dark green trees. Dazzling light bounced off the snow, making it hard to see.

She, Alex, and Sophie stood in the middle of a snow-covered road. Plain wooden buildings with tall fronts lined both sides. Some buildings were only half-finished. Between the buildings were snow-capped tents.

"What kind of a place is this?" Mattie wondered.

"Yippee!" Alex exclaimed. "We're back in the Wild West!"

Mattie pointed to a group of men standing in front of a clapboard building across the street. A sign over the door read, Restaurant. The men goggled at them as if they had seen the kids fall out of a spaceship in the sky.

"This place is wild, all right," said Mattie. "But I'm not sure if we're in the West. Those guys don't look like cowboys."

The men had on boots and parkas made of stitched hides and fur. They had scraggly beards and wore dirt-encrusted jeans. Their hair was shaggy, as if they'd cut it without looking in a mirror.

"Let's go talk to them," Mattie said. "We need to find out where we are and then figure out what our mission is."

They crossed the road and stopped in front of the group.

"Hi." Mattie gave her friendliest smile.

A man with a blue knit hat gawked at her.

"Where'd you three come from?" the man asked. "We didn't see you come into town."

Mattie worried whether he was curious about their shiny modern jackets. Sophie's was purple and had a cartoon cat on it.

"Uh . . . we just got here," Mattie hedged.

"I don't see no mule or sled dogs," said the man.

An enormous man with hands like hams stepped forward. Unlike the others, this man was dressed in a suit topped with a long wool overcoat. A thick, gold watch chain swagged across his stomach. Instead of a beard, he sported a drooping walrus mustache.

"Don't mind Old Pancake," the huge man said. "He's been mining in the Klondike so long, he doesn't know how to act in town."

"We aren't all lucky like you," said Old Pancake. "Anyhow, I get to town right often. But I haven't seen any young'uns for months."

The others murmured in agreement.

Now Mattie knew why the men were staring at them. Where on earth were they? Why weren't there any kids in this town?

"I suppose your father is in the Yukon looking for gold too?" the big man said to the kids. "Is he getting supplies in Dawson City?"

"This is a city?" Alex glanced skeptically at the board buildings and tents. "How come there aren't any—"

Mattie poked him before he could say "movie theaters or arcades."

"We just got over a fever," she said, inventing an excuse. "And we can't remember where we are. What state is Dawson City in?"

The big man guffawed. "This isn't the United States, little lady. It's Canada! The Yukon Territory."

"Some days I wish nobody had discovered gold up here," said Old Pancake. "It's hard work, mining a claim. 'Course, Big Alex wouldn't know anything about that." He nodded at the big man.

"Your name is Alex?" Alex asked. "It's my name too!"

The man bowed. "Alexander McDonald, at your service."

"Alexander Chapman, at your service," Alex said. "These are my sisters, Mattie and Sophie."

The huge man grinned at Mattie and Sophie. "Folks around these parts call me Big Alex."

"Or King of the Klondike," another man put in. "Tell the young'uns how you bought Thirty Eldorado for a sack of flour and a slab of bacon."

"Big Alex has more claims than anybody," Old Pancake said. "That's why we call him King of the Klondike."

Big Alex twirled his mustache. "The gold bed in Thirty Eldorado brought out five thousand dollars a day."

Mattie was confused. Gold bed? Claims? What were they talking about?

"How can you sleep in a gold bed?" Sophie asked. "Isn't it hard?"

Big Alex gave a booming laugh.

"A gold bed is a vein—or streak—of gold in the creeks around the Klondike River," he explained. "Ever since people found out gold was discovered here, they've come from all over to stake a claim and make a fortune."

"You didn't happen to bring in a newspaper, did you?" Old Pancake asked Mattie.

She shook her head.

He sighed. "I haven't seen a newspaper in so long, I forgot what year it is."

Big Alex slapped Old Pancake on the back. "It's 1897. Did you forget the month too?"

"No," said Old Pancake. "My old bones tell me winter's almost here. And a big snow is coming."

Sophie piped up, "I love snow." Then she began singing "Jingle Bells."

"Not now," Mattie whispered, nudging her.

Ignoring Mattie, Sophie sang through the

second verse. Then she gave a little curtsy. Mattie wondered when her shy little sister had become such a ham.

"Are you children entertainers?" Big Alex asked Mattie.

Mattie blushed. "Um . . ."

"Yes," Alex broke in. "We're the Famous Chapman Children. We'll put a show on for you guys if you want."

"Alex!" Mattie glared at her brother. "We can't—"

But before she could finish, Sophie stepped up on the stairs of the clapboard building. She faced the men and smiled shyly.

"This is Ellsworth," she said, holding up her stuffed elephant. "She's my best friend in the world. I'm going to sing to her."

Sophie held Ellsworth in both arms and began rocking the stuffed elephant.

"Rock-a-bye, Ellsworth, in the treetop," she sang. "When the wind blows, the cra-a-dle will rock. When the bough breaks, the cra-a-dle will fall. And down will come elephant, cra-a-dle and a-a-l-l-l-l."

The men clapped enthusiastically. Some wiped their eyes. Big Alex blew his nose loudly into a red handkerchief. Then he and the other men tossed shiny yellow lumps at Sophie's feet.

Mattie bent to pick up one. The lump felt smooth and cool. Gold! She gathered the nuggets and put them in her pocket.

Ales stepped up next. "I can't sing so I'll tell jokes. Knock knock."

No one answered. The men glanced at each other, puzzled.

"Who's there?" Sophie shouted.

Alex looked relieved. "Police!"

"Police who?" Mattie said.

"Police let us in. It's cold out here! Ha ha!" Alex laughed loudly.

Now the men caught on and laughed too. They tossed nuggets, which Alex scooped up.

"That's a good one!" said Old Pancake, slapping his leg.

"I think it stank," said a voice. A boy about Mattie's age stood at the back of the crowd. He wore a heavy knit sweater and stiff jeans caked with dirt. A fur-lined hat with turned-up ear flaps was pulled over his blond hair.

He frowned at Alex, then stomped away.

# - 4 -

# Klondike Mike

Mattie felt her temper flare. "Hey, what's your problem?" she called out, stomping after the boy. "Is that any way to treat new people in town?"

"It's the way I treat people in show business," the boy said with a sneer. He walked over to a large sled parked by the side of the building.

Mattie had never seen a sled like this one. It had long runners made from peeled saplings. Rope-lashed sticks supported two top rails. The rails and the runners extended beyond the sled's frame, like handlebars and foot rests. The sled was piled with paper-wrapped packages.

A big black-and-white dog was harnessed to the sled. When the dog saw the boy, he jumped to his feet and barked once in greeting. Several packages tumbled off the sled and into the snow.

"Ho, Mountie." The boy stooped to pick up the packages.

"I thought that was you," Big Alex said to the boy. He, Alex, and Sophie had followed Mattie. "I see Mountie is raring to go today."

"Ooooh," Sophie said. "He's so cute! Can I pet him?"

"Yeah," the boy replied. "He's big, but he's friendly."

*Friendlier than you are*, Mattie thought. She was a little nervous when Sophie kneeled to hug the big dog. But the dog licked her cheek with his pink tongue.

"You've done a fine job training him," said Big Alex. "That dog will be worth his weight in gold when the snow starts flying."

"He's worth more than gold to me now," the boy said. "Pa's waiting, so I'd better get a move on."

"Tell your father I said hello." Big Alex nodded at Mattie. "Glad to meet you children. I'll be back when you put on your regular act."

With the packages restacked, the boy stepped on the runners sticking out the back of the sled. The top boxes dropped off once more.

Alex stooped down to pick one up.

"Thanks," the boy said.

Mattie glared at her brother. Why was Alex helping this mean boy?

Alex murmured, "Trust me. It's a guy thing." He stood up and turned to the boy. "Why don't you let us carry some of those packages?"

The boy stared at Alex. "You want to lug supplies all the way to Henderson Creek?"

"Sure." Alex shrugged.

"It's a long way," the boy said. "You entertainers aren't used to hard work."

Mattie's temper flared again. "You don't know anything about us! We can work as hard as you. We ran an inn all by ourselves!" She didn't admit they were innkeepers for only one day.

"We don't mind hard work," Alex said, giving Mattie a sharp look.

"All right," the boy said grudgingly. "I could use some help."

Mattie and Sophie each picked up a package.

The boy stepped on the back of the sled, gripped the handlebars, and called, "Mush!" Mountie trotted down the street, pulling the sled.

"I'm Alex Chapman," Alex said, jogging to keep up with the sled. "These are my sisters, Mattie and Sophie. What's your name?"

"Mike Harding," Mike replied. "In camp I'm nicknamed Klondike Mike."

"What camp?" asked Alex.

"Where me and Pa have staked our claim. Fifty-five Henderson."

"I don't get this stuff," Mattie said. "Big Alex talked about Thirty Eldorado. What are you talking about?"

Mike shook his head. "You're a real greenhorn, even for a rusher."

"In English," Mattie said. "What's a rusher?"

"You're a rusher if you and your family rushed up here to find gold, same as me and my pa. Where are your folks, by the way?"

"They're . . . building an igloo," Mattie replied in desperation. Traveling back in time wasn't all fun and games. Answering questions was sometimes tricky.

"An igloo!" Mike laughed. "Everybody builds a cabin or lives in a tent."

"What about the gold?" Alex said.

"You must know about the men who discovered gold in Rabbit Creek, off the Klondike River," Mike began.

"In the river?" Mattie broke in. "I thought you dug gold out of a mine."

"Gold can be in rivers too. It's mixed in with regular gravel and rocks." Mike went on.

"Anyway, these men found a lot of gold—great big nuggets—and they took a boat to Seattle earlier this summer."

"How do you know all this?" Mattie asked.

Mike gave her a withering look. "Because my pa and me lived in Seattle. We happened to be on the dock when the boat landed. The miners got off carrying sacks of gold! One man lugged his gold in a suitcase. It was so heavy, the handle broke."

"Wow," said Alex.

"It gets better," said Mike. "Next thing we know, practically everybody in Seattle is heading for the Yukon. Once the story hit the newspapers, people all over the United States were making a mad dash up here."

Mattie glanced back at the town they were leaving. "But there doesn't seem to be that many people here. I mean, we didn't see anybody but those men at the restaurant. And you."

"That's because most people didn't get here in time," Mike said. "Pa read an ad in the newspaper. It said the gold in the Yukon is as thick as sawdust, just lying on the ground. Pa's store wasn't doing good, and him and me have been kind of down since Ma died a few years ago."

Mattie felt a pang. She was sorry he didn't have a mother. She decided to be nicer to Mike.

Mike stopped to adjust Mountie's harness. He brushed packed snow from between the dog's paw pads.

"Pa and me were lucky. We sold the print shop right away and bought tickets for the first steamship out. We had to buy a lot of supplies, enough food to last us a year." He stepped back on the sled and gave Mountie the command to take off.

"A year!" Mattie pictured buying shopping carts filled with boxes of cereal, loaves of bread, jars of peanut butter, and packages of cookies. "Where'd you buy that much stuff?"

"Pa went to Cooper & Levy Pioneer Outfitters. He bought buckets and shovels and chisels and candles and frying pans and boots and canvas and overalls. The pile was higher than me!" Mike measured to the top of his head. "We got on the *Queen*. It took six days to sail from Seattle to Skagway."

Alex giggled. "To where?"

"Skagway, Alaska. Didn't you come through there?"

"Yes," said Mattie. "I mean no."

"You must have come through White Horse Pass, then," Mike said. "You still would have seen the mess along the beach in Alaska. People everywhere, supplies everywhere. We came over Chilkoot Pass."

Alex started to laugh at the name, but Mike cut him off. "It was mountain of ice and snow. Somebody carved fifteen hundred steps up the steep side. Pa tied me to him so I wouldn't slip and fall. There were so many people climbing above and below us, I wouldn't have fallen far. I had to wear snow goggles to keep from going blind."

Mattie realized he was describing the scene on the postcard. He must have written the message too, about their dangerous trip.

"But you made it over," said Alex.

Mike snorted. "We had to climb it almost every day for two months."

"Why?" Mattie asked, astonished. Once sounded bad enough.

"Because we had to get our supplies

here! Horses and mules can't climb up a mountain of ice. When we got on the other side, we sat down on a packet of supplies and slid down to the bottom." He grinned. "One man carried crates of cats over the pass. He was crazy."

"What's he going to do with all those cats?" asked Sophie.

"Sell 'em to the miners," said Mike. "The Yukon is a lonely place. A lot of people would pay good money for a house cat. But that man and his cats are at Lake Bennett, like everybody else."

"I'm confused," Mattie said. "Where's Lake Bennett?"

Mike shook his head. "I don't know how you got here. In a hot-air balloon, I guess. Lake Bennett's about five hundred miles from Skagway to Dawson City, most of it by water. Most rushers get stuck at Lake Bennett."

"But you and your father got here," Alex said.

"That's because Pa hooked up with another fellow. He said if we hurried up and built a boat, we'd get up the Yukon River before it froze solid. So we cut down trees and slapped together a boat." Mike's blue eyes widened. "That was some trip! We shot through a canyon and steered through rapids. I was mighty scared!"

"I would be too," Mattie said. "When will the man with the cats and those other people come here?"

"Not till next spring, when the river thaws."

Mattie realized Mike and his father couldn't leave until spring either. "Are you homesick?" she asked.

"A little. I miss my friend Herb more than anybody." Mike stopped again. "I have to let Mountie rest. He's pulling a pretty heavy load."

Mountie's perky ears twitched when he heard his name.

"He has such neat markings," Mattie said, "like he's wearing a mask. What kind of a dog is he?"

"Malamute." Mike took a hunk of reddish brown meat from a pouch around his waist. He fed it to the dog. "Dried salmon. Pa and me eat bacon and hardtack, but this dog eats the best. He's a trained sled dog, not like the mongrels most men brought."

"People brought dogs too?" Sophie wanted to know.

"You need dogs to pull sleds," Mike said. "The guidebooks said to bring any dog over forty pounds. On the steamship, I saw all kinds of mutts. Most of those dogs were useless. They can't take these Yukon winters. A malamute can."

Alex patted Mountie's head. "How did you get Mountie?"

"One of the miners sold his claim. Since he was going back home, he decided to sell his dog too. I bought him and trained him." Mike rubbed Mountie's ears, then climbed back on the sled. The dog took off over the snow.

Mattie was tired. She wouldn't admit to Klondike Mike in a million years that her arms ached from carrying the bulky package and her legs hurt. He would say she was a puny city girl or something.

"How far are we going?" Sophie asked. Mattie was worried about her. Sophie was carrying the lightest package. But it was still a long walk for a five-year-old.

"Right over that hill," Mike told her. "See the smoke from the campfires?"

They crested a snow-covered ridge. Down below, a wide stream bubbled over rocks. All along the streambed, men kneeled or stooped, swirling water in metal pans. Others dug gravel with shovels. The men all wore dirty clothes and grim faces.

Mattie thought that hunting for gold would be fun, like searching for buried treasure. But these men did not look like they were having fun. They looked tired.

"How long have you and your father been here?" she asked Mike.

"A month."

"That long? Boy, you must be rich," Alex said. "How much gold have you got so far?"

Mike gave Mattie and Alex a level stare. "None. Not one single flake."

"None?" Alex lifted his eyebrows. "I thought gold was lying on the ground, thick as sawdust."

"That's what the advertisement said." Mike's tone was heavy with disgust. "But they were wrong."

Then Mattie knew their mission. She, Alex, and Sophie had been sent here to help Klondike Mike and his father find gold.

# 5

# Worth More Than Gold

Mike unhooked Mountie and pulled the sled along the ridge by the crossbar that attached the harness to the sled. The kids followed him to a rough cabin built in the shelter of a sweeping spruce tree.

As Mike parked the sled, a tall, thin man opened the door. Mattie noticed he had Mike's blond hair and blue eyes. She figured he was Mike's father.

"You're back," he said to Mike. "I was

getting worried. It's clouding up. That big snow might be coming soon." He glanced at Mattie, Alex, and Sophie. "Looks like you picked up some new friends."

"Yes, sir," Mike replied. "This is Mattie and Alex and Sophie. Meet my pa."

Mr. Harding nodded at them. "Are you here with your folks?"

Mike jerked his thumb at Mattie and Alex. "They're performers."

Mike's father grunted. "Ah, well, we don't have time for entertaining 'round here. Not when there's work to do. I'll finish unloading these things. Mike, head down to the claim."

"Can't we help you?" Mattie asked. She wanted to get started on their mission.

Mr. Harding looked skeptical.

"All right," Mr. Harding said. "Mike, since your new friends are so anxious to work, take them too."

"Oh boy!" Alex cried. "We're going to look for gold!"

Mike led them down to the stream. Mountie trotted by his side, his plumy tail curled over his back.

"Our claim is Fifty-five Henderson," he said. "That means Pa staked the fifty-fifth claim along this creek."

Mattie nodded. Mining was starting to make sense. "Big Alex staked the thirtieth claim on Eldorado Creek?"

"Yeah," Mike replied. "Everyone does placer mining here. That means we don't dig for gold in underground mines. The gold is in the creeks and gravel bars, so we pan for it or use the rocker."

He walked down the stream, past men who washed rocks in tin pans or pumped the handles of strange-looking wooden contraptions, then stopped at a crudely lettered sign that read, *Harding Number 55.*

"This is it." Mike waved toward a strip of gravel jutting into the rushing stream. "Five hundred yards along this bank. You'd think we'd find some gold. I'll teach Sophie to pan. Alex, you and Mattie work the rocker."

"This thing?" Mattie stared at a box built on top of a slanted wooden trough. Below the trough sat a bigger wooden box. A bucket hung from a wooden handle at the top.

"That's our rocker," Mike explained. "You pour rocks and water in the box on top. The bottom of the box is covered with mesh. The mesh catches big rocks but lets little ones through."

Mattie nodded. "Then what?"

"The water goes down the trough. Small gravel and rocks are trapped here." Mike rapped the slanted bottom of the trough.

"Sand and water pours through the hole in the side of the trough into the big box."

"So how do we work it?" Alex wanted to know.

"One of you will dump water in the top box," Mike said. "And the other will pump the handle. That rocks the box. Holler if you see anything shiny and yellow. That's gold, you know," he said to Mattie.

Then he took Sophie down to the gravel beach. Mountie bounded after them, zigzagging in and out of the water.

"Mike makes me so mad!" Mattie said. " 'That's gold, you know.' He acts like girls are stupid. Go get some rocks. I'm going to find gold before he does!"

Alex picked up the bucket and went down to the stream to scoop up gravel. He stumbled up the hill, sloshing water. Then he tipped the bucket into the top box.

Mattie pumped the wooden handle up and down. As the box rocked, pebbles rattled down the trough to settle at the edge. Water and sand flowed through the hole into the big box below.

"See anything?" he asked.

She sifted through the pebbles but caught no telltale flash of yellow. She turned toward Mike and Sophie, who were hunkered down at the edge of the gravel bar.

"Mike!" she called. "We don't see any gold. Now what?"

"You think gold is going to jump out of the river?" he called back. "Keep working!"

Alex trudged back down to the creek for more water. He dumped bucket after bucket into the rocker. Mattie pumped the handle until she thought her arm would drop off.

"You the Hardings' new partners?" asked a voice.

Mattie looked up. A man with black hair and a bushy black beard leaned on a shovel. Next to him, a dog with black and white patches wagged a scraggly tail.

"No," Mattie replied. "We're just . . . helping out. I'm Mattie. This is my brother Alex. Our little sister is down there with Mike."

"Folks call me Blueberry Pete," the man said. He laughed at Mattie's expression.

"It's because when I find a blueberry bush, I eat 'em all."

"Is that your dog?" Alex asked.

"Yeah," Pete answered. His dog thumped his tail. "Smitty is a good boy but not much use in this territory."

"He's not a malamute," Mattie said.

"No, just a mutt," said Pete.

Smitty scratched furiously behind one floppy ear.

"My partner and I are working fifty-six. Next claim over." Blueberry Pete pointed downstream to another man with black hair and a bushy black beard. He was panning at the edge of the creek. A hint of red peeked out from his mud-covered pant leg. "That's him—Gravel Curly."

"He looks just like you!" Mattie said.

Blueberry Pete laughed. "Yeah, that's what everyone says. But you'll always know

Curly by his red socks. He wears 'em every day."

Mattie waved, but Gravel Curly didn't wave back.

"He's not too friendly," explained Pete. "Curly's been in the territory for years. He doesn't talk to anybody hardly." He lowered his voice, even though his partner was too far away to hear. "Curly's got gold fever."

"What's that?" Mattie had never heard of that disease.

"Oh, gold fever is bad. Most of us want to strike it rich and go home. But some fellows like Curly get prospecting in their blood. He's followed gold rushes for years—California, Colorado. And now the Yukon."

"Doesn't his family mind?" Alex wondered.

"Curly doesn't have any family," Pete said. "All he thinks about is gold. He's got a cabin back in the woods somewhere. Old Curly is looking for the mother lode."

"The what?" asked Mattie.

"Mother lode. All the gold in these creeks has to come from one source. The gold has washed down from one big vein of gold ore. Whoever finds that vein will be the richest man in the world."

"Why hasn't anybody found it yet?" Alex asked.

"It's not easy finding gold here. It's freezing cold most of the time." Blueberry Pete swung his shovel over his shoulder. "Well, better get back to work or Curly will yell at me for lollygagging." Clucking his tongue at his dog, he went back to his own claim.

"Let's trade jobs," Alex told Mattie. "I'll wiggle that little handle and you carry a billion tons of rocks."

"No way." Even though her arm was sore, she figured hauling water from the creek was worse. "I never knew looking for gold was such hard work."

Alex was staring at something in the distance.

"Planet Earth to Alex," Mattie said.

Then she saw the man running along the edge the creek. He was much younger than Blueberry Pete. His thick, wavy blond hair blew wildly in the wind.

"Gold!" the man yelled excitedly. "I found gold!"

# 6

# Fool's Gold

Blueberry Pete and Gravel Curly scrabbled up the bank to join the young man. Mike and Sophie threw down their pans and scurried to the scene. Mountie galloped in front of them. Mattie and Alex rushed over too.

Soon the young man was surrounded by prospectors. Mountie and Smitty milled around everyone, barking and wagging their tails.

"Did you say you found gold?" Blueberry Pete demanded. "Where?"

The young man gasped for breath. "Downstream about half a mile! I just stuck my shovel in the gravel and came out with gold!"

"Look!" The blond man pulled a small leather sack from his coat pocket and emptied its contents into the palm of his hand.

Mattie stood on tiptoe to see the glittery chunks of yellow metal.

Gravel Curly picked up one of the chunks between his thumb and forefinger and held it up to the light.

"Fool's gold," he announced in a scratchy voice.

"Fool's gold?" said the young man. "What's that?"

"Pyrite," Blueberry Pete explained. "Looks like gold. Not worth a cent."

The young man stared at the rocks in his hand. "But . . . but . . ." he sputtered.

"You aren't the first person to be fooled by pyrite," said Gravel Curly.

The prospectors turned away and returned to their claims.

"Here." The young man gave Sophie the shiny yellow rocks.

Mountie pushed his black nose into the

stranger's hand. The young man laughed.

"A genuine sled dog," he remarked. "Who does he belong to?"

"Me," said Mike.

"Fine animal," the young man said. "He's worth a fortune. Who are you prospectors?"

"I'm Klondike Mike Harding," Mike said. "My pa and me are working Fifty-five Henderson."

"We're helping," said Mattie. "I'm Mattie. This is Alex and that's Sophie."

"Pleased to meet you," the young man said. "I'm Jack London."

Mattie had a funny feeling she had heard that name before.

"Well, we'd better get back to work," Mike said.

"And I guess I'll go back to my claim," said Jack. "Or maybe I'll go fishing!" With a jaunty wave, he strode off in the direction he had come, and the kids headed back to the Hardings' claim.

Just then Mr. Harding appeared.

"Any luck?" he asked Mike.

Mike shook his head.

Walking over to the rocker, Mr. Harding checked the pebbles in the bottom of the rocker's trough. His lips thinned in a tight line.

"We've been here a month now and we haven't found a speck of gold. This claim is a skunk!" he declared.

Mattie was puzzled. "A skunk?"

"That means there's no gold here," Mike replied. "Pa, we could hunt for another spot. A better one."

"We don't have time. The old-timers say the big snow is on its way. We'll have to stay here this winter and go home in the spring. If we can afford it."

"You might find gold tomorrow," Alex said hopefully. "We'll keep working."

Mr. Harding gave him a wry smile. "Thanks, young man. Come eat, everyone. Dinner's ready."

The kids started to follow Mr. Harding up the hill to their cabin.

Mike glanced around. "Wait. Where's Mountie? He was just here." Mike whistled.

"He probably wandered off," Mattie said. "You know how dogs are."

"Not my dog. He never leaves me. And he always comes when I whistle." Mike whistled again. "Mountie! Come on, boy!"

They waited. No dog appeared.

"My dog! Something has happened to my dog!" Mike's voice sounded strained, as if he was trying not to cry.

"Maybe he strayed off for a while," said Mr. Harding. "He'll come back. Let's go eat before the food gets cold."

"He would never run off," Mike said, sniffling.

Mattie was struck by a sudden thought. She had been completely wrong about their mission! She, Alex, and Sophie weren't sent back to the Yukon to help the Hardings find gold. They were sent to help find Mike's dog!

# 7

# The Right Mission

"I love Mountie more than anything except Pa," Mike confided to Mattie as they walked up the hill toward their cabin.

"We'll find him," she promised. Finding a dog had to be easier than searching for gold on a "skunk" claim.

The Harding's cabin was constructed of peeled greenish logs. Moss had been stuffed between the logs. One small window was made of glass jars bonded by dried mud.

When Mattie stepped inside, she nearly turned her ankle. The floor was made of logs that were hard to walk on. Her eyes stung from the wood smoke. The cabin smelled of burned bacon, stinky boots, and wet wool from socks drying over the woodstove.

A plank table and two splintery chairs stood in the center of the room. Bunk beds had been built into one wall. Crude shelves held sacks of flour and rice. Piled on the floor were buckets, crates, and boxes overflowing with matches, rice, candles, nails, tins of pepper, and cans of beans.

Mattie and the others took off their coats. It was almost as cold inside the cabin as it was outside.

Mike's father lifted an iron pot off the stove and scraped brown beans onto tin plates. He added chunks of scorched meat from an iron skillet. Mike opened a tin canister and took out large, brownish crackers.

"Pull up some crates to sit on," Mr. Harding said, setting the plates on the table.

Mattie sat down and picked the large cracker off her plate. "What is this?"

"Hardtack," Mike replied. "This is what we eat every day—beans, bacon, and hardtack."

"No vegetables?" Mattie asked. Her mother had said everyone needs to eat vegetables. Even though Mattie didn't like some vegetables, she would get sick of nothing but beans and bacon.

Mike snorted. "Do you see any gardens in the snow?"

Flushing, Mattie nibbled at her beans. The bacon was too salty. The cracker was hard all right, and it didn't have much taste. She wished she had her burned shortbread.

The wind whistled through the dried moss chinked between the logs. Mattie wondered how Mike and his father would survive all winter in a drafty cabin, eating beans and salty meat.

"Done." Mike dropped his fork on his plate and jumped up. "We're going to look for Mountie, Pa."

"Don't get caught by the dark," his father warned.

They bundled up again and hurried outside.

Mike called and whistled for Mountie, but the dog didn't answer.

"Let's go," he told the kids. "We have to find him before dark."

"Sophie is too little to walk far in the cold," Mattie said. "And we can't leave her here."

"She can ride in the sled." Mike unfolded

a fur rug from the bottom of the sled.

Sophie climbed in. Mike tucked the rug around her, then hooked Mountie's harness over his shoulders.

"Mush!" Sophie said to Mike.

They walked past the boundary of the Harding claim and along the edge of Henderson Creek, with Mike pulling the sled.

Mike stopped at Fifty-six Henderson. Gravel Curly was pouring water into their rocker while Blueberry Pete pumped the handle. Pete's black-and-white dog dozed nearby.

"Have you seen Mountie?" Mike asked them. "I can't find him."

Curly didn't look up. "No," he growled.

But Pete stopped pumping. "Let's see . . . last time I saw Mountie was when that young fella showed us his pyrite."

"Jack London?" asked Mattie.

"Yeah, that's him." Blueberry Pete said.

"Back to work," Gravel Curly barked out at Pete.

"Sorry, kids," Pete said, and he started pumping again. "Good luck."

"Jack London took my dog!" Mike exclaimed to the kids.

"Blueberry Pete saw Mountie with Jack London," Mattie said. "That doesn't mean Jack London took him. Mountie could have followed him."

"Maybe." Mike tightened his jaw.

"Last time we saw Jack London, he said he was going back to work his claim," Alex said. "Maybe we could find him and ask if he's seen Mountie."

They moved down the creek, halting at each claim. All the miners knew Mountie, but no one had seen him or Jack London lately.

Discouraged, Mike slumped in the

harness. Mattie was afraid he'd start crying. She didn't think Mike was a sissy. In fact, she thought he was really brave to have climbed all those icy steps and shot the rapids on a dangerous river. Even though he made her mad sometimes, she didn't want him to feel so bad.

"We're doing this wrong," she said. "We should be looking for tracks. Mountie didn't just vanish into thin air. He must have left tracks in the snow."

"Mattie's right," said Alex. "Let's fan out so we can cover more ground."

"Don't go out of sight of each other," Mattie cautioned.

Mike pulled the sled with Sophie along the edge of the stream, Alex headed up the hill toward the woods, and Mattie searched along the bank above the stream.

She saw dozens of boot prints, but no

paw prints. What if they couldn't find Mike's dog? The Yukon Territory covered hundreds of miles. Mountie could be anywhere.

"Hey!" Alex cried, several yards away. "Over here!"

Mattie crunched through the snow into the woods. Mike hauled the sled up the hill.

Alex was standing by a big pine tree. He pointed to a series of paw prints crisscrossing in front of the tree. "I bet these belong to Mountie!"

Sophie shook her head. "Nope."

"Curved paw pad, four toes, that's a dog all right," said Mike. "It has to be Mountie!"

"It isn't," Sophie insisted. Mattie wondered what Sophie knew that nobody else did. Sometimes her sister had strange ideas that turned out to be true.

"I'm not listening to a little girl," Mike said. "I want my dog back and this is the only clue we have so far."

"Then we'll follow the tracks," said Mattie. "They go that way."

With Mike in the lead hauling the sled, the kids slogged up the hill. The tracks traveled down the other side of the hill, around trees and boulders. Then the prints broke off.

Mattie stared at the snowy ground. "The tracks are gone! What happened?"

"Maybe somebody picked Mountie up and carried him," Alex said.

"No, we'd see shoe prints." Mattie checked behind an ice-covered bush. "I found the tracks again! Maybe the dog jumped over this bush."

On the trail once more, the kids struggled through deep snow. The trees grew closer, making it hard for Mike to pull his sled between them.

"Look!" Alex said.

A small cabin was perched on a ridge, overshadowed by enormous boulders. The paw prints led them around the back of the cabin, circling to the front. Then the tracks faded away by a snow-dusted boulder.

Mattie couldn't find the trail again. "Mountie must be inside," she said.

Mike and Alex approached the front door. Sophie clambered out of the sled and followed Mattie.

"If he hears my voice, he'll bark," said Mike. "Mountie! Hey, boy!"

But all they heard was the hoarse croak of a raven flying overhead.

"Maybe he's asleep," Alex said. "Let's try the door."

Mattie knocked. As she did, the wooden door swung inward. "It's open." She pushed the door wider and stepped inside. The others followed.

The cabin had a tiny bottle-glass window that didn't let in much light. She didn't see Mountie anywhere.

"He's not here," Mike said, disappointed.

As her eyes adjusted to the dimness, Mattie noticed a pair of bunks, a table, and chairs. Bags of flour lined the floor, and clothes, pans, and other supplies hung from nails on the walls.

"The stove is still warm," said Alex, testing the woodstove. "The guy who owns this cabin was here not too long ago."

Mattie wandered over to the table. It was littered with papers and books. She flipped through a dull-looking book called *Paradise Lost*. The papers were more interesting. The wide-spaced, sprawling handwriting was difficult to read, but she thought it was part of a story. Crumpled, torn papers were scattered like leaves on the floor around the table.

Mike glanced out the window. "It's getting dark."

"We haven't been gone that long, have we?" said Alex.

"It's the weather," Mike replied. "The sky is real gray. You know that big snow everyone keeps talking about? I think it's finally coming."

They were all quiet a moment. Mattie had never heard such silence. It was as if the whole world had disappeared.

In the crisp stillness, she heard another sound, like boots crunching in the snow.

"That's not all that's coming," she said. "Quick! Hide!"

# 8

# The Call of the Wild

Before Mattie could move, the door opened and Jack London scuffed inside.

When he saw the kids, his eyes widened and he grinned. "If I knew guests were coming, I would have baked a cake." Then his grin faded. "Now tell me what you all are doing in my cabin."

"Your cabin?" Mattie said.

"Yes, mine. I share it with my buddy. Anyway, I live here and you don't." He crossed his arms. "I'll ask again—why are you here?"

"Mike's dog is missing," Sophie answered. "We're looking for him."

"There's dog tracks all around your cabin," Mike accused.

"You thought I took your dog?" Jack said.

Mike stuck his chin out. "Blueberry Pete and Gravel Curly said they saw you with Mountie."

"I didn't take your dog," Jack said gently. "I may not be a good prospector, but I haven't stooped to dognapping yet."

Something clicked in Mattie's mind. She remembered where she'd seen Jack London's name—on the cover of the book she fetched for her father, *The Call of the Wild*! The author's name had been spelled out in icicle-shaped letters. Her father had said the book was about a kidnapped dog!

Could they believe Jack London?

"Are you a writer?" she asked him.

He stared at her. "Yes. How did you know that?"

"You like dogs, don't you?"

Jack pulled off his hat. "Of course I like dogs. But that doesn't mean I go around stealing them. I saw enough of that in San Francisco."

"People swiped dogs there?" asked Alex. "How come?"

"When news of gold in the Yukon hit San Francisco—that's where I'm from—everybody went crazy. The list of supplies included a dog over forty pounds. Dog owners had to lock up their pets because rushers would steal any good-sized mutt."

Mike nodded. "It was like that in Seattle too. I have to find Mountie now, before the big snow hits."

"I'll help you look," Jack said. "Show me the tracks you found."

Mattie led the way outside, with Jack right behind her. Sophie hopped in the sled. Mike and Alex tugged the sled into the woods.

Mattie showed Jack the paw prints circling the cabin. "They end here," she said, stopping at the set of deep prints by the boulder.

Kneeling, Jack picked up a twig and brushed the snow away from the paw print. "These aren't dog tracks. They're too big. This is a wolf."

"A wolf!" Mattie said. "There are wolves around here?"

"Wolves, bears, reindeer, moose—those wild animals belong to this place more than we do." Jack stood up. "They know how to live in the wild. We don't."

"But the tracks end," Mike said. "Where did the wolf go?"

Sophie pointed to the top of the boulder. "Up there."

"Sophie's right," Jack said, walking around the huge rock. The kids followed him. "See? The tracks start up again on this side. The wolf must have jumped on top of the boulder, probably to throw you children off his trail. Wolves are smart. He figured out you were after him."

Mattie shivered. What if they had caught up to the wolf?

"These prints aren't frozen yet," said Jack. "That means they are fairly fresh. The wolf could be close."

Just then a bone-chilling howl shattered the glassy stillness of the forest. Mattie felt the cry all the way down her spine. It was the eeriest sound she had ever heard in her life.

She never wanted to hear it again.

"He's close," Jack whispered. "Stay by me."

Mattie grabbed Sophie's hand. "Is he going to come after us?"

Before Jack could reply, the wolf's call was answered by distant barking.

"That's Mountie!" Mike cried. "He's in danger!" He lurched forward, but Jack London pulled him back.

"You're in more danger than your dog," he said. "Normally wolves are shy, but if he's hungry enough, he might attack you."

"We have to rescue his dog," said Mattie. "We can't just leave him."

Mike threw her an admiring glance.

"I'll come with you," Jack said, breaking off a sturdy branch from a tree. "I can drive the wolf off if I have to."

The wolf howled again, setting off a

frenzy of barking.

"We'll follow the sound of your dog's barking," Jack said to Mike.

They plowed through the snowy forest. It was tough going. Brambles clawed their clothes. They had to scramble over fallen logs and scale rocks. The sled became wedged between trees.

Mattie's feet were freezing. Every time she ducked under a limb, snow slithered down her neck. She was glad Sophie was bundled in the fur rug.

The barking grew louder as they waded through blue-tinted drifts.

"Look!" Alex exclaimed. "Another cabin!"

Tucked under a rocky outcropping was a ramshackle cabin. It seemed to be built into the side of the hill.

"Who would live way back here?" Jack wondered.

Mattie spotted a pair of red wool socks hanging from a tree. She knew instantly who owned the cabin.

"This must be Gravel Curly's place," she said. "Blueberry Pete told us Curly had a cabin in the woods someplace. And Curly always wears red socks."

Jack was examining the ground. "There are other tracks. Boots. The wolf.

And . . . a dog."

"Mountie!" said Mike.

Immediately the barking grew frantic.

"He's in there!" Mike unharnessed himself and stumbled through the snow to the cabin.

"You three go with him," Jack told Mattie. "I'll keep an eye out for the wolf. He's not too far, I'm sure." He stalked off through the woods, carrying his stick.

"Mike!" Alex cried. "Wait for us!"

Mattie and Alex pulled the sled up to the cabin.

"Let's leave it around the side," Mattie said in a low voice. "Gravel Curly's probably still working his claim. But just in case somebody is in there, we don't them to know we're here."

She and Alex dragged the sled around the corner. Sophie clambered out and they hurried to the front door.

Mike had his hand on the latch.

Mattie grabbed his arm. "Wait! We'd better make sure Mountie is alone."

She crept up to the window, standing on her tiptoes to peer inside. Before she could see anything, the front door opened with a bang.

# 9

# Surprise in the Cabin

Mattie whirled, expecting to see Gravel Curly.

Blueberry Pete grinned at them from the doorway. His dog, Smitty, stared at the kids. He wasn't barking, but the barking sound continued from inside the cabin.

"That's my dog in there!" Mike yelled at Pete.

Blueberry Pete laughed. "If you want him, come in." His tone became serious. "Now."

Mattie knew he wasn't kidding. Clutching Sophie's hand, she walked into the cabin with Mike and Alex. Blueberry Pete followed them inside and firmly closed the door. He left Smitty on guard outside.

Like the other cabins, this one had built-in bunk beds and shelves for supplies. But the wooden floor was crusted with dirt, and a tottering heap of empty tin cans towered to the ceiling.

A dog sprang up from where it had been lying by the stove and hurled itself at Mike.

"Mountie!" Mike cried with joy. He hugged the dog's furry neck. Mountie wriggled with happiness.

Mattie was relieved that Mountie was safe, but what would they do now? Would Blueberry Pete let them walk out? Maybe if they acted casual, they would throw him off.

"We've been looking all over for Mike's

dog," she said lightly, though inside she quaked. "Thanks for finding him. We'll be going now."

She strolled toward the door, but Pete sidestepped in front of her. He seemed bigger than ever.

"Not so fast," he said.

"You didn't find Mountie," Mattie said. "You stole him, didn't you?"

"And nobody saw me," he admitted.

"Not even that young fella who found fool's gold."

"You tried to make us think Jack took Mike's dog," said Alex.

"Why did you do it?" Mattie asked Pete, stalling for time. She needed to think of a way out.

Blueberry Pete uncoiled a rope hanging from a nail. "Curly has an idea where the mother lode might be, but we won't be able to look till next spring. Food and supplies in Dawson City cost an arm and a leg. This dog is worth a lot of money. Curly and me need that money."

"You can't sell my dog!" Mike yelled. "I won't let you!"

Pete stalked over and started to knot the rope around Mountie's leather collar. Mike tried to stop him, but Pete pushed him away.

"You won't be able to do anything about it." Pete tugged Mountie away from Mike. "I'm locking you in."

"You can't keep us here forever!" Alex said.

"Not forever. Just a good long while," Pete said with a wicked grin. "Maybe a real long time. Nobody knows where Curly's cabin is."

*Jack London does*! Mattie thought. But Jack was off tracking the wolf. He couldn't help them.

"The big snow should start tonight," Pete went on. "Curly and me will be in Dawson by then. Might be days before anybody finds you." He sounded unconcerned.

Mattie gasped. "You can't do that!"

When the blizzard struck, she figured their footprints would be covered. They could be trapped for a week. Or longer!

She, Alex, and Sophie could use the spy-glass and go back home, but they couldn't leave Mike behind. And they couldn't take him into the future with them. They had to accomplish this mission.

Blueberry Pete dragged Mountie to the door. The dog strained against the rope leash, barking in protest.

Mattie thought fast. The sled was just around the corner. Blueberry Pete didn't know it was there. If they could distract him, they could make a break for it and use the sled as a getaway car.

But what would nab his attention? Mattie shoved her hands into the pocket of her parka. Her fingers touched something hard and smooth. Suddenly she knew how to distract the prospector.

Pete unlatched the door. Whining, Mountie tangled the rope around Pete's legs. While Pete unwound the leash, Mattie whispered her plan to the others. They nodded in agreement.

Then Mattie yelled, "Look!" She flung one of the nuggets from her pocket across the room.

Blueberry Pete spun around and made a dive for the bright nugget skittering across the floor.

"Go!" Mattie called to the others.

The kids bolted through the door. Mountie broke away and loped by Mike's side. Pete's dog, Smitty, lunged at them, but Mountie bared his teeth and the smaller dog scuttled off.

"Hurry!" Alex said. He leaned his weight against the door to keep Blueberry Pete inside.

With nimble fingers, Mike harnessed Mountie to the sled. "Get in! Mountie can't pull four so I'll run behind. Mattie, you'll have to steer."

"But—" She couldn't steer a sled!

Sophie and Alex tumbled into the sled. "Mattie!" yelled Alex.

The cabin door slammed open.

"Get back here!" Blueberry Pete thundered.

Mattie hopped on the back of the sled and shouted to Mountie, "MUSH!"

Blueberry Pete tore outside, his face twisted in anger, his boots churning up snow.

Mountie didn't move. The dog seemed frozen like a block of ice.

Mattie closed her eyes. It was all over.

# - 10 -

# Sophie Strikes It Rich

"You'll never get away!" Blueberry Pete bellowed. His voice sounded dangerously close.

Mattie clenched her eyes shut. She expected to feel Pete's hand clamp her shoulder any second.

Instead, she felt the runners glide beneath her. She opened her eyes.

"Mush!" Mike ordered.

This time Mountie leaped forward.

The dog's powerful muscles rippled as he gathered his feet and bounded into the woods. The sled whooshed over the snow. Mike ran alongside them.

Mattie glanced back. Blueberry Pete was still chasing them, but he was falling behind. The miner stopped and shook his fist in frustration.

"He's giving up!" Mattie said.

"Go, Mountie!" cried Alex.

As the dog zipped through the woods, Mike told Mattie which commands to call.

"Gee," she yelled and Mountie shifted to the right to miss a tree. She cried, "Haw!" and Mountie pulled to the left.

After a few minutes, Mike said, "Easy!" The dog dropped his pace to a fast trot.

"Hey!" said Alex. "How come we're slowing down?"

"Mountie is pulling a heavy load," Mike

replied. "And he's just one dog, not a whole team. Blueberry Pete won't catch up with us now."

Mattie didn't hear the man yelling after them anymore, only the sound of cold air rushing past her ears. She loved flying through the dark forest and wished they had a dog at home instead of grumpy old Winchester. That cat would never pull a sled.

"Hey!" Sophie said. "There's Jack!"

Jack London sprinted toward them, waving his arms.

"Whoa!" Mike told Mountie. The dog slowed to a stop.

"You found Mountie!" Jack said. "Was he in the cabin?"

Mattie told him the story. Jack's eyes narrowed when she was finished.

"I've heard that people will do anything to find gold, but this is the worst," he declared. "Pete and his partner in crime will not get away with this."

"Did you find the wolf?" Alex asked.

"Yes!" Jack brightened with excitement. "I walked under a ledge and felt this large presence above me. I looked up and there sat the wolf. He stared at me and I stared at him. Neither of us blinked. I think he hypnotized me. I have never seen such a wonderful creature."

From his expression and the way he talked, Mattie knew that Jack would never forget the wolf. Maybe he would get the idea from their rescue of Mountie to write that book about a dog in the Yukon.

"We need to get back to camp," Jack said. "Mike, your father is probably frantic with worry. And you Chapmans—"

"Our parents know where we are," Mattie said hastily. "Sort of."

Jack gave her a strange look. "Let's hurry back to camp. Mike, your dog looks pretty tired."

"I can walk," Alex said, climbing out of the sled.

"Me too," said Mattie. "But Sophie should ride."

Mike nodded. "You kids are tougher than I thought." He punched Mattie on the arm. "Especially you."

"Thanks," she said, rubbing her shoulder. "I think."

Lavender shadows tinted the snow by the time they reached Henderson Creek. It was early evening.

Mattie spied Mr. Harding talking to a group of miners as they crested the last hill. Mike's father ran to meet them.

"Where have you been?" he demanded. "I was getting together a scouting party."

"We found Mountie," Mike told his father. "Blueberry Pete had dognapped him. He and Gravel Curly were going to sell Mountie!"

"Sell a boy's dog?" Mr. Harding shook his head. "That's pretty low."

"Gold fever makes men do crazy things," Jack said.

"Well, they aren't getting away with it." Mr. Harding petted Mountie's head. "I'm going to report those two scoundrels to the Royal Canadian Mounted Police the next time I'm in Dawson. Meanwhile, let's use the last of the daylight and go work the claim."

"I'll help," said Jack.

At Fifty-five Henderson, Jack manned the rocker handle while Mr. Harding poured water into the top box.

Mike, Mattie, Alex, and Sophie trooped down to the water's edge. Mike gave them each a tin pan.

Mattie bent down and dredged up rocks with her pan. The water was freezing!

They worked for a while, dipping and digging. Mattie could see how people caught gold fever. She swished pan after pan of gravel, always hoping for a glimpse of yellow metal.

"Mattie." Sophie tugged on Mattie's sleeve. "Look what I found."

Mattie tipped her pan, examining pebbles before they slid over the edge. "Just a sec, Soph."

"It's a pretty rock. See how shiny it is?" Sophie held up a large gold nugget.

Mattie dropped her pan. "Ohmygosh! Sophie's found gold! Hey, everybody!"

Alex tossed his pan in the air. He and Mike raced over. Jack and Mr. Harding came running.

"May I see?" Mr. Harding asked Sophie.

She nodded and gave it him. His face turned pale.

Jack whistled. "That's a fair-sized nugget! Worth at least five hundred dollars."

"Yee-ha!" Mike whooped. "We've struck gold!"

In no time, men from other claims swarmed around. They exclaimed over the wondrous size of the nugget.

"Mike," Mr. Harding said. "What do you say we head back home?"

"But we sold the shop. We don't even have a place to live," Mike said.

"We'll make out somehow," his father said.

Mattie reached into her pocket. She pulled out the nuggets Big Alex and the other men had tossed to Sophie.

"Take these," she said. "We don't need them."

Sophie handed over her sack of fool's gold. "This too."

Alex bent down and fiddled with his boot laces. Mattie knew her brother too well.

She leaned over and whispered, "Give it up, Alex."

"Not my gold," he whispered back.

"You can't take it with you!"

Alex dug reluctantly into his pocket and handed the rest of the nuggets to Mike's father.

"Are you children sure?" Mr. Harding said.

"Well—" Alex began.

"We're sure," said Mattie, giving him a little kick.

A wide smile split Mr. Harding's face. "We'll buy a new shop," he told Mike. "And we'll have enough left to buy a little house!"

Mike jumped up and down and Mountie

started barking. Soon everyone was talking and clapping Mr. Harding on the back.

"Now," Mattie said to Alex, "we've finished our mission."

Alex slipped the spyglass from his parka and held it by one end. Sophie clutched the middle. Mattie grasped the other end, hoping they would disappear before Mike and the others missed them.

She felt the spyglass grow warm under her fingers and it felt wonderful! She was tired of being cold.

She closed her eyes and let flecks of gold, white, and green dance behind her eyelids. The snowy ground seemed to drop away beneath her feet.

*Whump*!

Her boot hit the tower room floor. Mattie opened her eyes. Alex and Sophie appeared beside her.

Morning sun flowed through the long, narrow windows. Mattie was hot inside her heavy parka. She shed her coat and boots and helped Sophie take hers off.

A car door slammed outside. Mattie ran to the window overlooking the driveway.

"It's Mom!" she said. "She's back early."

"Maybe Dad called her," Alex said.

"I'm glad we don't have to be innkeepers anymore," said Mattie. "That's one job Mom and Dad can take back!"

"Get the letter," Alex said, putting the spyglass away in the desk. "Let's see what the Travel Guide wrote us."

Mattie retrieved the envelope from the cubbyhole in the desk. She glanced out the window again. Her mother was hauling groceries from the trunk of her car.

"We have plenty of time to read the letter," Mattie said. "Let's go help Mom first."

Alex nodded. "I'm going to fold the laundry."

"And from now on, I'll set the table without being asked," said Mattie. "At least our chores aren't as hard as panning for gold!"

Alex swiveled the bookcase-panel and crawled through on his hands and knees.

Mattie grabbed their jackets and hats and pushed them through the opening ahead of her. As she began to crawl through, she looked back over her shoulder.

"Sophie? Don't you want to come help Mom?"

"Yeah. In a second." Sophie bent over a drawer in the desk.

Mattie thought she saw a slip of yellowed paper flutter from her sister's fingers—a rumpled scrap with scrawling handwriting.

No. Maybe her eyes were still snow-dazzled.

Dear Mattie, Alex, and Sophie:

How did you like being prospectors? You learned how hard it is to find gold. Yet people will go anywhere and live under the harshest conditions to get rich quick.

America has a long history of gold fever. In 1848, gold was discovered in California. Three hundred thousand people joined the rush. Few of the "forty-niners," as they were called, made their fortunes.

Ten years later, gold was discovered in the Colorado Territory. Prospectors cried "Pike's Peak or Bust" as they raced to the Rocky Mountains.

In 1896, Canadian Robert Henderson discovered gold along a creek off the Klondike River. Shortly after, George Carmack panned gold in another creek. More prospectors joined them. Most returned to the United States in July 1897, staggering off ships with pickle jars, suitcases, blankets, and bags filled with gold. That triggered the next wave of gold fever.

One hundred thousand people, mostly from the United States, flocked to the Klondike region in Canada's Yukon Territory, an area the size of Texas. Those who made it found that most of the Klondike claims had already been staked. Ill-equipped for the harsh winters, people fell ill to snow blindness and scurvy, a disease caused by lack of vitamin C.

Several child performers trekked to the Yukon to entertain homesick miners. Nine-year-old Margie Newman sang, danced, and acted, earning the nickname "Princess of the Klondike." Crystal Brilliant Snow was only three when she began her career. Crystal became a teacher and served two terms in Alaska's territorial government.

Big Alex McDonald fascinated everyone. He was more interested in running gold mines than the gold itself. In his home, he kept 45 pounds of nuggets in a bowl. He told visitors to take as much as they wanted. Once he presented a golden bucket of nuggets to an official's wife, saying, "Take it. It's trash."

As you know, one of the "rushers" was twenty-one-year-old Jack London. He had tried to be a writer, but no one would publish his stories. Craving adventure, Jack bought two thousand pounds of supplies and headed north. He stayed in a cabin that winter, though he didn't find gold. In the spring, he went to Dawson City, sick with scurvy. He made friends with two men who had a mongrel dog.

Jack and his friends explored the Yukon River. Jack kept a journal and later wrote books and stories from those experiences. The sled dog Buck in The Call of the Wild was based on the dog in Dawson City. He also wrote White Fang, which is about a dog that is part wolf, and the stories "To Build a Fire" and "White Silence."

In the 1960s, a cabin was found in the Yukon. Jack London, Miner, Author, Jan. 27, 1898 was carved on one wall. The cabin was dismantled and two replicas were built, one in Dawson City and the other in Jack London Square in Oakland, California.

The territory of Alaska was rich in gold too, and prospectors swarmed to Juneau and Nome. The last rush took place in 1902 in Fairbanks.

As for the Klondike mother lode, it has

never been found, though people are still looking for it more than a hundred years after the Yukon gold rush.

Your next adventure will be a rocky one, but not golden!

Yours in time,
Mr. Cutright

# TIME SPIES MISSION NO. 8
## TRACK A TREASURE

On this trip, you followed a trail of tracks in the snow. Learning to identify and follow different types of tracks is a skill you need as a spy.

One way to practice this skill is to create a fun treasure hunt for your fellow Time Spies. Start out by picking three or more locations. Then make up clues. Your clues can be simple, such as, "Go to the maple tree on the corner." At the maple tree, hide another clue. At the last place, hide your prize: a sack of "gold" chocolate coins or, even better, one of Jack London's books.

To make the hunt more fun, "sign" your name with a dog track stamp you make yourself!

### WHAT YOU NEED:

Water-bottle cap
Small piece of craft foam
Scissors
Glue
Ink pad

## WHAT YOU DO:

1. Trace or draw the paw print on your piece of craft foam.
2. Cut out the paw pad and each of the toes.
3. Arrange the paw pad and toes on the bottle cap so they form the correct shape of a dog's paw print.
4. Glue the foam pieces to the cap.
5. When the glue is dry, use your stamp on your ink pad.
6. Write each clue and sign it with your stamp.
7. Hide the prize.
8. Let the treasure hunt begin!

## Don't be chicken!
## Read the whole series!

### Fowl Language
June 2008

### Fine Feathered Four Eyes
June 2008

### Poultry in Motion
September 2008

And the feathers keep flying in 2009!

For more information visit:
Supernaturalrubberchicken.com